Dear Parent:
Your child's love of rea

Every child learns to read in a differe
speed. Some go back and forth betwe _____ and read
favorite books again and again. Others read through each level in
order. You can help your young reader improve and become more
confident by encouraging his or her own interests and abilities. From
books your child reads with you to the first books he or she reads
alone, there are I Can Read Books for every stage of reading:

SHARED READING
Basic language, word repetition, and whimsical illustrations,
ideal for sharing with your emergent reader

BEGINNING READING
Short sentences, familiar words, and simple concepts
for children eager to read on their own

READING WITH HELP
Engaging stories, longer sentences, and language play
for developing readers

READING ALONE
Complex plots, challenging vocabulary, and high-interest topics
for the independent reader

ADVANCED READING
Short paragraphs, chapters, and exciting themes
for the perfect bridge to chapter books

I Can Read Books have introduced children to the joy of reading
since 1957. Featuring award-winning authors and illustrators and a
fabulous cast of beloved characters, I Can Read Books set the
standard for beginning readers.

A lifetime of discovery begins with the magical words "I Can Read!"

Visit www.icanread.com for information
on enriching your child's reading experience.

A Family for Lewis

Meet the Robinsons: A Family for Lewis Copyright © 2007 Disney Enterprises, Inc. RADIO FLYER is a registered trademark of Radio Flyer, Inc. and is used with permission. All rights reserved. No part of this book may be used or reproduced in any manner whatsoever without written permission except in the case of brief quotations embodied in critical articles and reviews. Printed in the United States of America. For information address HarperCollins Children's Books, a division of HarperCollins Publishers, 1350 Avenue of the Americas, New York, NY 10019. www.icanread.com

ISBN-10: 0-06-112470-2 — ISBN-13: 978-0-06-112470-9

❖   First Edition

DISNEP
MEET THE
ROBINSONS
A Family for Lewis

Adapted by Sadie Chesterfield

Illustrated by The Disney Storybook Artists

Designed by Disney Publishing's Global Design Group

HarperCollins*Publishers*

Meet Lewis. He is an inventor.

Lewis never knew his parents.

He lives in an orphanage

where none of the kids have parents.

Today he is showing a new invention.

Maybe the man and woman will like it

and want to adopt him!

But the invention splatters goop,

and the couple runs away.

Sometimes Lewis is sad.

Will he ever find a family?

Up on the roof of the orphanage,

Lewis has time to think.

He wonders what his mother was like.

Then Lewis gets an idea.

He will invent a Memory Scanner

to help people remember things!

I will remember my mom and find her.

We will be a family! he thinks.

Lewis stays up all night
to work on his Memory Scanner.
Now he can bring it
to the science fair!

At the busy science fair,

Lewis sets up the Memory Scanner.

Lewis really wants it to work.

Then he will remember his mom

and have a family of his own!

But then something strange happens.

A boy named Wilbur appears and says,

"I am a special agent from the future."

"I don't believe you," says Lewis.

Lewis thinks that Wilbur is crazy.

Then the Memory Scanner falls apart!

The science fair is ruined,

and so is Lewis's dream

of being a great inventor

and finding a family.

Wilbur follows Lewis up to the roof.

Lewis throws away his invention plans.

At first Wilbur hides,

but then he sees that Lewis is upset.

"Don't give up!" he tells Lewis.

Lewis will not listen to him.

So Wilbur does something

to make Lewis listen.

He pushes Lewis off the roof!

But Lewis lands in the air.

What is holding him up?

It is an invisible Time Machine!

Wilbur takes Lewis to the future
in the Time Machine.
The boys see flying cars
and moving sidewalks.

"This was all invented by one man,"

says Wilbur.

"He is called the Founder of the Future.

Lots of his inventions failed, too,

but he never gave up," says Wilbur.

Wilbur gives Lewis a hat

to cover his old-style hair.

That way, no one will know

he is from the past.

Lewis decides to explore Wilbur's house.

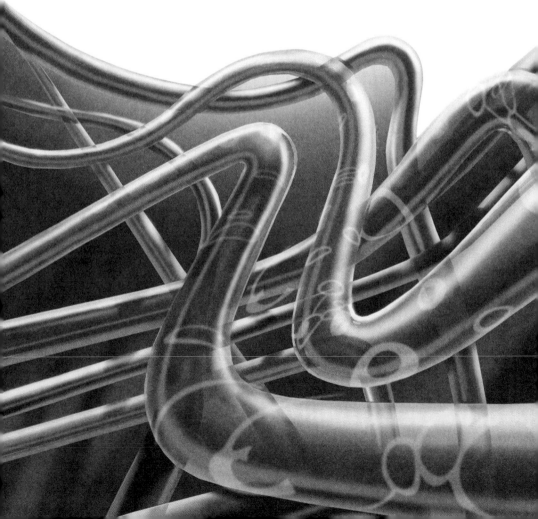

He gets caught in a Travel Tube!

A gust of wind carries him along

a curvy, clear tube.

It is scary!

Wilbur's mom, Franny,
invites Lewis to dinner.
It is the strangest and best dinner
Lewis has ever had.

Uncle Gaston starts a food fight,
and the whole family joins in!
Lewis would love to belong to
a family like this!

The Robinsons like Lewis, too.

"Do you want to be a Robinson?"

they ask Lewis.

"Yes!" Lewis says.

But Wilbur says, "No!"

Wilbur has to stop his family
from making a mistake!
He shows everyone Lewis's hair.
Now they know he is from the past.
Lewis's haircut makes him look
just like Wilbur's dad, Cornelius.
In fact, Lewis will grow up to be
Cornelius Robinson in the future.

"You can't stay in the future,"
Franny tells Lewis.
Lewis has to go back to the past
so he doesn't mess up the future!
He has to grow up to be Cornelius.

At last, Lewis meets Wilbur's dad.

He is the same person as Lewis,

only all grown up.

Franny is angry with Wilbur

because he brought Lewis from the past.

Now Cornelius knows what happened.

Lewis must return to the past! Fast!

But first, Lewis goes on a tour

of Cornelius's laboratory.

It is filled with great inventions.

Cornelius shows off his favorite one.

It is the Memory Scanner!

"It really did work!" Lewis exclaims.

He has to get back to the science fair

so he can fix it.

Lewis returns to the science fair
and repairs his Memory Scanner.
One of the judges tries it out.
She remembers her wedding,
and it shows up on the monitor.
The Memory Scanner works!

The judge is named Lucille.

She will be Grandma in the future.

She is married to Bud Robinson.

He will be Grandpa in the future.

Lucille and Bud adopt Lewis
and change his name to Cornelius.
Now Cornelius can grow up
to be Wilbur's dad. Bud and Lucille
will be Grandma and Grandpa.
Lewis has finally found
a family of his own.